Magazine Mania

Follow the Glitter Girls' latest adventures!
Collect the other fantastic books in the series:

Caroline Plaisted

Magazine Mania

■SCHOLASTIC

Scholastic Children's Books,
Commonwealth House, 1-19 New Oxford Street,
London WC1A 1NU, UK
a division of Scholastic Ltd

London ~ New York ~ Toronto ~ Sydney ~ Auckland
Mexico City ~ New Delhi ~ Hong Kong

Published in the UK by Scholastic Ltd, 2003

ISBN 0 439 98176 X

Typeset by Falcon Oast Graphic Art Ltd
Printed and bound in Great Britain by Cox & Wyman Ltd, Reading, Berkshire

2 4 6 8 10 9 7 5 3 1

Chapter 1

"Right," said Miss Stanley, ticking off names in the register. "Everyone's here! Let's get going then!"

There was a buzz of excitement in the Glitter Girls' class at Wells Road School. It was Tuesday morning and they were all off on a trip to the town's newspaper offices.

"I've been looking forward to this for weeks," Meg said.

"Me too," agreed Charly. "I hope we get to meet some of the reporters."

"Do you think we'll see Sara?" asked Zoe.

Sara was a reporter on the paper and the Glitter Girls had met her when she had come along to the painting party the girls had helped to organize at the community hall.

"Hope so," said Flo. "But I'm really keen to find out how they design the pages and make all the words and pictures fit together. My sister says everything is done on computers – just like we do stuff at home on ours."

Before the Glitter Girls could talk any more, Miss Stanley called out to the class, "OK everyone! Coats on and in pairs by the door please. Amy – you can walk with me at the front. Gemma's mum is coming with us and she'll walk at the back." Miss Stanley looked round at her class. "I think Robert can walk with her. Ready everyone? Let's go!"

The Glitter Girls had been to the newspaper office in the centre of town lots of times but they had never been allowed to go into the offices behind the reception area before.

As soon as they got there the receptionist

gave everyone a badge to clip on to their school sweatshirt that read VISITOR.

"Mr Frost, our editor, is going to show you round," the receptionist explained. "Ah – here he is now!"

A tall man with grey hair arrived. "Well hello!" he said. "It's great to see you here, boys and girls, and to have the chance to tell you about how the newspaper works. Shall we go?"

"Yes!" everyone replied enthusiastically.

"First stop, editorial," Mr Frost said. "This way."

The class followed him into a busy office where lots of people were talking on the phone and working at their computers.

"This is where our reporters write their pieces," Mr Frost explained. "They get some of their news from people who telephone the paper to tell us about forthcoming events. But a lot of the time they have to go out and interview people to report the news."

"How do they remember what to write?" Zoe asked.

"Well, let's ask one of the reporters, shall we?" Mr Frost suggested. "Sara? One of our visitors has a question for you."

Sara swung round in her chair and smiled at the group.

"Sara!" said Charly, as excited as the other Glitter Girls to be seeing their friend again.

"Go Glitter!" Sara laughed, holding her hands in the air, just like the Glitter Girls always did. "So you're all here to find out how a newspaper is made, are you?"

"Yes!" the whole class answered at once.

"This young lady would like to know how you remember the information when you are out on an interview," Mr Frost explained.

"Well," said Sara, "usually I take my notebook with me and I write things down in a special writing called shorthand."

The boys and girls exchanged puzzled looks.

Sara smiled. "Shorthand is a way of making notes using symbols instead of words. Once you learn to write shorthand it's a really fast way of writing things down."

"Can we see what it looks like?" asked Joe, one of the boys in the class.

"Of course, here's an example." Sara passed her notebook around the group and, one by one, everyone looked, fascinated to see the squiggles and lines.

"This doesn't make sense!" said Flo.

"It does if you understand shorthand!" Sara laughed. "But there is another way of keeping a record. If I am going off to interview someone, I might take a special small tape recorder with me – like this one, called a dictaphone – and then I can just have a really good chat without having to write anything down." Sara held up a tiny black box. It was much smaller than any other tape recorder they had seen.

"So how do your notes and stuff get into the paper?" asked Cheyenne, from the back of the group.

"When I get back to the office, I write my copy – that's what we call the story – on the computer," Sara explained, pointing to her monitor where she was typing up an article. "Sometimes I might double check I've got the facts right with the person I interviewed. But Mr Frost has the final decision about what goes into the paper."

Mr Frost winked at them and smiled. "Any more questions?"

"What about the photographs?" Flo wanted to know.

"That's Brad's job," Mr Frost said. "Let's go down the corridor and find him."

Brad had a small office at the end of the corridor. Just like everyone else, he had a computer on his desk. But instead of having lots of words on it, there were photographs.

"How do you get photographs on there?" Robert asked.

Brad explained how he accompanied the reporters and took the photographs on a digital camera. When he came back to the office he loaded the photos on to the computer.

"Once we've chosen the photographs that we are going to use for all the stories, I write the captions and put those on to the computer along with the photographs," Brad said.

"What are captions?" asked Jessica, one of the Glitter Girls' friends.

"They're the words under the pictures to explain each photograph," said Brad.

"You mean the ones that tell you who's in the picture and how old they are?" Flo asked.

"That's right." Brad laughed.

"Thanks, Brad," said Mr Frost. "Now let's go downstairs to the design department and find out how the newspaper is put together."

"Yes!" said Flo, hurrying over to the stairs, eager to be first.

In the designers' room, a group of people were busily working away at computers.

"Wow! You've got loads of computers in this place!" said George.

"We have," agreed Mr Frost. "And these ones are used by Nina, Jamal, Petra and CJ."

"Hello!" the four of them said to the class.

"What do you do?" Hannah asked.

"We're graphic designers," Nina explained. "We design the newspaper. CJ and I get all the stories from Sara and the other reporters and the photographs from Brad, and then we design the way the pages look. We have to make sure there's enough space for all the words and that the pictures end up with the right stories."

"And I work with Jamal to put all the advertisements in at the back of the paper," Petra said.

"Can you show us how to do some design?" Flo asked, eagerly.

"Of course!" said Jamal.

It was great! The whole class spent the next half an hour learning how to use the computers. And all of them got the chance to help design a section of a real page from the newspaper.

"You'll have to look on Thursday to see what your finished work looks like," Mr Frost said. "Now –" he looked at his watch – "we'd better hurry up and go down to the print room and see some of the paper actually being printed!"

★ ♥ ★ ♥ ★ ♥ ★

The print room was really noisy! The Glitter Girls, along with all the rest of Miss Stanley's class, were introduced to Brian, who was in charge of all of the newspaper's printing presses.

Brian explained how the paper was fed into

the large printing press machines, and after the machine operator pressed more buttons on yet another computer, huge sheets of newspaper with all the articles, photographs and adverts that the designers had put together appeared. Then another machine sorted the pages into order and the finished newspaper arrived at the end.

All around them machines were hard at work. As the paper moved along the machines, people were checking that everything was working properly and nothing was getting jammed. Everyone was busy but they still found time to smile and say hello.

"But how can you be printing the newspaper already if Sara and Brad haven't finished their jobs?" Meg asked.

"And Jamal and the others haven't finished doing the design either!" said Flo.

"You lot are pretty smart, aren't you?" Brian laughed. "Actually, this isn't the newspaper we're printing today, it's the magazine section.

We can print that earlier in the week because it doesn't have news in it. It lists what's on in the town over the weekend – things like plays and concerts as well as giving details about cinema and television. Come on – let's go to the machine over there and you can all take home an early copy of the magazine."

"Excellent!" the whole class said at once.

Chapter 2

"Wasn't it good to see Sara again?" Meg said when the Glitter Girls were back at school, eating their lunch in the hall.

"She's got such a great job, hasn't she?" Charly sighed. "I'd love to have the chance to do her job for a while."

"Just give me Brad's job any day!" agreed Flo.

"Everything at the newspaper was interesting," said Zoe.

"Isn't it amazing the way the paper just whizzes through the machine and comes out looking like a magazine!" exclaimed Hannah.

"I know!" said Flo. "I'd love to have the chance to help make a magazine – it'd be such fun."

"Do you think Miss Stanley will ask us to write something in class this afternoon about our visit?" Zoe asked.

"Hey!" said Hannah. "Maybe we could design a page for a pretend newspaper about our visit!"

"That would be great," said Charly.

"Hmm," Meg said. Then a grin appeared on her face.

The other Glitter Girls recognized it at once.

"What is it, Meg?" Hannah begged.

"Yes – go on, tell us!" asked Zoe.

"Well, I was just wondering," Meg said slowly.

"About what?" urged Charly.

"About doing a page of a newspaper," Meg explained. "I mean, why should we only do one page when we could do lots?"

"Do you think we could?" said Zoe. "A whole newspaper this afternoon in class?"

"Actually," explained Meg. "I was thinking

that we could take longer than that. We could do it properly – you know, make it one of our projects!"

"Brilliant!" said Charly.

"Sounds cool to me!" agreed Zoe.

"It's about time we had another adventure!" said Hannah.

"But we haven't got the right computers and stuff at home, have we?" Charly pointed out.

"And who would we make a newspaper for?" Flo wondered.

"We could do a school magazine!" said Meg. "Ready for the end of term! Jack brought one home from his school last term. It was full of stuff about pop music and how all the sports teams had done."

"Do you think Miss Stanley would let us do one?" Zoe wondered.

"A magazine would be even more fun than a newspaper!" said Flo.

"Let's go and find Miss Stanley and ask," suggested Charly.

"Go Glitter!" her friends all agreed.

★ ♥ ★ ♥ ★ ♥ ★

"So you see, Miss Stanley, we thought we could get it done by the end of term!" Zoe explained.

The Glitter Girls had found Miss Stanley back in their classroom. She was busy getting things ready for the afternoon when the Glitter Girls arrived and told her about their great idea.

"Gosh – I never realized that a visit to the local newspaper would get everyone quite as enthusiastic as this!" Miss Stanley laughed. "A school magazine . . . it sounds rather a big project to finish by the end of term. There's only four weeks left, after all."

"But we could do it!" begged Charly.

"Yes – we could!" agreed Meg.

"If we all worked together as a team and

made it a joint project," said Flo, twiddling with her hair.

"Then we could have the magazine ready for everyone to take home at the end of term!" said Hannah.

"I'll tell you what, girls," Miss Stanley said. "I think it sounds like a good idea too. . ."

"Yes!" the five girls yelled at once.

". . .*but*!" Miss Stanley put her finger to her lips to get the girls to be quiet again. "But I still think it's too much for you to do on your own. After all, if it's a school magazine I think everyone would like to have something to do with it. I think we need to speak to Mrs Wadhurst about your idea. Tell you what, I'll try to catch her now, before lessons start. You wait here – I'll be right back."

Just a few minutes later Miss Stanley returned.

"What did she say?" asked Charly excitedly.

"Can we do it?" Hannah asked.

"Well, Mrs Wadhurst thought it was a great idea—" Miss Stanley began.

"Yay!" cheered Zoe.

"Wait a minute, Zoe," Miss Stanley said, laughing. "But she thought it was too much work for just you five, and I agree."

The girls sighed disappointedly.

"However," Miss Stanley went on. "She did suggest that if you were to have help from the rest of the school then she'd be happy to let you do it."

"Hurray!" Meg yelled, and the other girls joined in.

"She suggested we mention it in assembly tomorrow and then we'll have a meeting at lunchtime to see if enough children are interested. What do you think?" Miss Stanley looked at the Glitter Girls expectantly.

"Go Glitter!" the girls replied.

Chapter 3

The Glitter Girls were at the front of the queue outside their classroom after lunch the next day. And it was a long queue! Boys and girls from all the classes had come along to find out more about the school magazine that Mrs Wadhurst had told them about in assembly that morning.

After about five minutes, Miss Stanley came down the corridor from the staff room. She had a notebook in her hand, and looked pleased to see so many people waiting.

"Come on in and take a seat," Miss Stanley said, making her way to her usual chair at the front of the class.

"So," she said, picking up a notebook and

pen. "We're here to talk about doing a school magazine. We've only got about four weeks until the end of term. So, just like some of us found out at the newspaper office yesterday, we need to work as a team to get all the different jobs done."

"Bags I take the photos!" Flo volunteered.

"And can I interview someone?" Charly asked.

"I want to write about the football team!" said Georgios, who was in Year Six and the captain of the school team.

"Steady." Miss Stanley held up her hand, gesturing to everyone to quieten down. "Now let's not get in a mess even before we've begun. I need to write down everyone's tasks. By the end of this, we need to have sorted out how we're going to get the magazine done."

"Can I help with getting everything ready?" Meg asked.

"I was talking to Mrs Wadhurst about that over lunch," the girls' teacher said. "She thought it would be a good idea if I was editor of the magazine. But I'll need a deputy editor to help me out with everything. Do you think you could take on that role, Meg?"

"Yes please!" Meg grinned.

"Is there anything else that someone particularly wants to do?" Miss Stanley asked, looking around the group of eager faces. "We'll need drawings, photographs, stories, news . . . all sorts."

"Can I do a cookery piece?" asked Tony. Tony's dad ran a tea shop in town and everyone knew how delicious his cakes were!

"That would be great," said Miss Stanley, writing it down.

"Can we include stuff about fashion, clothes, hair – that sort of thing?" Hannah asked.

"Boys don't want to read about that sort of girls' rubbish!" Ollie grimaced.

"Well, what do they want to read about?" Zoe asked. Personally, she thought a fashion column sounded like a good idea.

"Boys like fashion, don't they?" said Miss Stanley. "And you boys are certainly just as interested in hair as the girls. I mean how many of you have got the latest David Beckham haircut?"

Ollie went red as he realized that he was one of them!

"We could have a girls' fashion column and a boys' one too," suggested Hannah.

"I'll do the girls' one!" said Amy.

"And I think Ollie should do the boys' – OK, Ollie?" Miss Stanley asked.

"If you like," Ollie said, shrugging.

As the meeting went on, Sue, who was in Year Three, asked if she could do a crossword puzzle.

"Good idea," everyone agreed.

"Can I do a piece about redecorating your bedroom?" Hannah asked. She loved everything to do with sewing and decorating.

"That's a really good idea!" said Amy.

"We haven't got anything about music yet," said Meg.

"I could write a report about who's passed any exams or played in concerts," suggested Claudia.

"Excellent," said Miss Stanley. "Why not include everyone who's done any kind of exam? You know, ballet, judo, drama – all of those things."

"OK," smiled Claudia.

"Can I do something about pop music?" Meg asked.

"You could do a column like the one they have in *Top of the Pops* magazine about the latest releases," suggested Ollie.

"I could go to the record shop in town and ask them to help me with it!" said Meg.

"Great," said Miss Stanley.

"Can I do a kind of news column?" Zoe asked.

"What sort of news?" wondered Flo.

"You know – stuff like Mrs Roberts having a

baby, the new drama club – oh, and Mr Green running the marathon," said Zoe. Mr Green was the school cook.

"You could call it 'What's Hot!'" giggled Tony, thinking he was just making a joke about Mr Green's school lunches.

"Actually, I like that!" said Miss Stanley. "I think it's a great name for a news column."

"I think we should include some more about our school," said Mitzi, who was in Year Six. "Maybe we could write something about the boys and girls who left at the end of last year – how they are getting on at their new schools."

"That's a great idea!" yelled Meg. "But maybe we shouldn't just keep it to people who left last year. I saw a programme on television a few weeks ago called something like 'Back to School' and it was about a group of school-friends who got together after ten years."

"Perhaps we could try and trace people who were at Wells Road!" suggested Charly.

"Loads of people still live round here," agreed Robert.

"Cool!" said Claudia. "I wonder if there's anyone famous who came here?"

Miss Stanley laughed. "Who knows? But it's a great idea!" she agreed.

"We've got lots of great ideas!" said Meg.

"Yes – and we'd better get going on them," said Miss Stanley. "Especially if we're going to get this magazine ready in four weeks! So – can you all go away and think about the task you've agreed to do? Then when we meet tomorrow you can tell us all what you're going to include for your bit."

Chapter 4

RAT-tat-tat!

"Who is it?" asked Zoe from behind her bedroom door, later that afternoon.

"GG!" hissed her four best friends as they pushed open the door and tumbled inside.

"Take a seat," Zoe said, finding a space for herself on her bed alongside Meg.

The other girls fell on to floor cushions and tucked into a plate of sandwiches.

"This magazine's going to be great, isn't it?" Charly said.

"I can't wait to do the design stuff," Flo grinned.

"There's a lot of work to do," Meg said, pulling her notebook from her pocket and flipping it open.

"We'll do it," said Hannah confidently. "After all, there are so many people helping, aren't there?"

"I never thought so many people would want to do it," Zoe sighed, hugging her knees to her chest.

"We'll have to make sure it's really good," Meg said determinedly.

"I can't *wait* to do my bedroom makeover," said Hannah excitedly.

"What sort of stuff are you going to put in the article?" Meg asked.

"Oh – making ordinary cushions into great cushions, customizing picture frames . . . that sort of stuff."

"Sounds good," said Flo. "It'll have to be illustrated. It's going to be fantastic to learn how to design magazine pages on the computer."

"The whole thing's going to be great," Charly said. "Writing stories, interviewing people – just everything!"

And her friends agreed.

★ ♥ ★ ♥ ★ ♥ ★

The next meeting of the magazine committee was held at breaktime the following day.

"Glad to see you all came back." Miss Stanley smiled at the group of boys and girls. "So who's got something to report?"

A sea of hands shot up!

"My goodness," Miss Stanley said. "Who's going to start? Ollie – why don't you tell us what you've been thinking about for your boys' fashion column."

"I thought I'd write about sports clothes and the latest trainers," Ollie said. "That's what boys like wearing."

"Sounds good." Miss Stanley nodded enthusiastically.

"And will there be pictures to go with it?" Flo asked. "You can't have a fashion page without pictures, can you?"

"Someone could draw the pictures, couldn't they?" Charly suggested.

"Nice one!" Ollie smiled. He hadn't thought about illustrating the article until now.

"Tell you what," said Miss Stanley. "Why don't we go through all the ideas we had yesterday? Then we can work out what illustrations or photos we're going to need and ask some of the other boys and girls if they can draw some of them for us."

"Yes," said Amy. "Then we can choose the ones that look the best."

"Good idea!" said Meg.

"I think we've all forgotten something though!" warned Flo.

Everyone looked at her, wondering what it was.

"At the newspaper they were working to a special plan, weren't they? The designers had worked out where everything was going to be put in the newspaper and then they made sure it was all going to fit."

"Well remembered, Flo," said Miss Stanley. "I think it was called a flat plan."

"Sounds like we need to do one," said Amy, who was sitting at the back of the meeting.

"Come on then, let's get started," said Miss Stanley. "Flo – do you think you'd like to help out with that flat plan?"

"Yes!" Flo grinned and rushed off to get a piece of paper.

★ ♥ ★ ♥ ★ ♥ ★

They only had about twenty minutes left, but everyone got down to work straight away and eventually they managed to find a home for everything they wanted to include in the magazine. Flo had worked out that they had about twenty pages to fill.

"I'll draw up the list of pictures that we need at lunchtime," Meg offered.

"Thank you, Meg." Miss Stanley smiled. "Then why don't you take it along to the office and ask if Mrs Packer will have time to type it up and deliver it to the classes this afternoon?"

"OK," Meg nodded. "But what shall I say it's for?"

"What do you mean?" Georgios asked. "It's for the school magazine!"

"Yes I know that," said Meg. "But what's it called?"

In all the excitement to work out what was going to go in the magazine and where, no one had remembered that the magazine needed a name!

"We've got to call it something special!" Charly said.

"Why not *Wells Road School Magazine*?" Tony asked.

"Oh wow, that's really exciting – I don't think," said Claudia.

"That's it!" said Zoe.

"What? *Wells Road School Magazine*?" said

Amy, puzzled. "I thought we wanted to call it something exciting."

"We do!" said Zoe. "*Wow!* That's exciting!"

"*Wow!*" said Flo. "That's good!"

There were murmurs of approval around the room.

"Looks like we've found the title then!" said Miss Stanley, smiling.

"Can we tell Sara at the newspaper about it?" said Charly. "After all, she might be able to help us find some of the old pupils we're looking for."

"Yes!" said Hannah. "She might!"

"Excellent idea, Charly," said Miss Stanley, and the others nodded.

"We'll tell her!" said Meg, looking at her friends. "We could go after school today!"

"Go Glitter!" her four best friends agreed.

"That's very kind of you, girls," Miss Stanley said, looking at her watch. "Right, shall we meet up again tomorrow at lunchtime?"

★ ♥ ★ ♥ ★ ♥ ★

"Don't be too long, girls," Mrs Fisher warned as she dropped the Glitter Girls off at the newspaper office later that afternoon. "Lily and I will be back in about half an hour."

"OK!" the girls all called at once.

Once they were inside, the receptionist recognized them.

"I know those uniforms!" She grinned. "How can we help you this time?"

"We wondered if we could see Sara?" Meg asked.

"I'll just see if she's in." The receptionist smiled and pressed some buttons on her phone. She chatted to someone and then said, "You're in luck."

Fortunately, Sara didn't keep the Glitter Girls waiting for long.

"So what have you come to tell me about?" she asked.

Between them, the five girls explained all about their school magazine and the things that everyone had promised to write for it.

"And we've decided to call it *Wow!*" Meg explained.

"That sounds great, girls," said Sara.

"We're going to see if we can find out what's happened to some of the old pupils who left school ages ago," Hannah said.

"We want to find out what they are doing now," said Zoe. "Maybe some of them are even famous!"

"Do you think you could help us?" Charly asked.

"Hmm," Sara said, suddenly scribbling things down in her notebook. "Yes, I'm sure I can – I think I'll write something for this week's paper! Do you think I could come in to get a photo of your magazine group first thing tomorrow?"

Hannah, Charly, Zoe, Flo and Meg looked at each other and smiled with pleasure.

"Go Glitter!" they all screamed at once.

Chapter 5

There was another meeting of the magazine contributors on Thursday after school.

"Look at this!" said Miss Stanley, holding up the front page of the newspaper that had come out that morning.

WOW! CALLING ALL OLD WELLS ROAD PUPILS! read the headline of the article at the bottom of the front page. Beside it, there was a great picture of all the boys and girls holding their arms out and saying, "Wow!"

"That's fab!" said Meg.

Miss Stanley read some of the article aloud to everyone: " '*The school's young editorial team are looking for former pupils. So, however long ago you left, please write in to tell them what you are doing now and if you have any special memories – including photos – of your time at Wells Road.'* That should stir lots of memories!" Miss Stanley said. "And I love the photo!"

"What are we going to do now though?" Meg asked.

"Well – I need to find out who's already started on their section of the magazine," Miss Stanley said. "Also, I want to give you all this timetable I've worked out." She handed everyone a sheet of paper and they all started to read it.

"Any questions?" Miss Stanley asked.

"When can I start putting everything together on the computer?" Flo wanted to know.

"As soon as possible," their teacher replied. "But we need to find out if everyone thinks they can stick to this timetable first. Amy, you go first – how are you getting on?"

The Glitter Girls met up in Meg's house after school that day. They were having a great time braiding each other's hair and making friendship bracelets.

"So who are you going to interview for the magazine, Charly?" Flo asked.

"I don't know," Charly said as she started to weave a tassel of silver charms through Zoe's hair.

"Well, you'll have to think of someone soon," said Meg.

"I know!" Charly sighed. "But the only person I can think of at the moment is Mrs Wadhurst and, well, I don't want to be rude, but she's not that exciting, is she?"

"I know what you mean," agreed Hannah. "You really need someone who people don't know much about."

"Difficult one," said Zoe. "But you're bound to think of someone."

"Maybe there's someone who's coming to do

a play at the theatre where Hannah's mum works?" Meg suggested.

"I could ask my mum," said Hannah.

"That's a brilliant idea," agreed Charly. "Please can you ask her tonight?"

"Yes, sure," Hannah said, smiling at her friend.

"I wish we could write a feature on hair and make-up," said Flo, admiring Zoe's hair.

"But Amy's doing the fashion column. . ." Hannah confirmed.

"Yes – but she's not going to write about hair braids, is she?" said Charly. "We could write about how to make different designs with braids and plaits. Maybe even some body-art stuff."

"Maybe we could persuade Miss Stanley to add another column to the magazine," suggested Flo, eagerly. "I'd have to change that plan I made."

"But even if there is enough space," Meg said, thinking aloud. "How will we know what people want us to write about?"

"We could ask them to tell us!" said Hannah.

"That's it!" said Meg, suddenly stopping the plait she was doing in Hannah's hair and finishing it off with a sparkly purple hair tie. She pulled her notebook out. "We could ask other girls in school if they have any questions – you know, about how to do braids and special make-up effects."

"Then we could answer them!" grinned Charly.

"And we could call it 'Go Glitter'!" suggested Flo.

"Go Glitter!" all her friends agreed.

On Friday at lunchtime, Mrs Packer, the school secretary, rushed into the magazine meeting waving a letter in the air. They were in the middle of looking at all the great things people had already delivered to school about their own school days. There were photos and letters –

even old newspaper cuttings and concert programmes.

"Sorry to interrupt but I know that you will want to see this!" Mrs Packer said as she sat down next to Hannah. "It's a letter from a Mrs James," she continued. "She lives just outside of town, but she used to live in Mount Crescent a few years ago and she's written to tell us that her daughter used to be a pupil here."

"So?" Ollie said, getting impatient to find out what was so special.

"So," Mrs Packer went on. "Mrs James's daughter is called Janine and she's the editor of a magazine you might have read called *Glitz*."

"Hey, cool!" said Amy. "*Glitz* is great!"

Mrs Packer grinned. "So that's a really interesting ex-pupil you can write about in *Wow!* Now, I must leave you to it – you've probably got lots to talk about."

Suddenly the room was filled with the noise of the excited chatter of every girl in the room.

All of them read *Glitz* – it was the best magazine there was!

Mrs Wadhurst stood up to leave, handing the letter to Miss Stanley.

"Now, everyone!" Miss Stanley smiled, trying to get their attention. "Let's keep looking through all these other letters and see what else we can find."

"Wow . . . Janine James used to come here," said Charly excitedly as the Glitter Girls were hanging out in the playground afterwards. There were only about five minutes left before the bell went.

"I wonder what she's like?" Zoe said.

"She's probably really cool," said Hannah.

"And I bet she wears great clothes!" said Meg.

"Yes," sighed Charly. "And she must have interviewed all kinds of famous pop stars and models."

She thought for a moment. Suddenly she jumped into the air and yelled enthusiastically, "I know! Why don't I interview Janine? She'd be perfect for the magazine!"

"Hey, that's a really great idea, Charly," said Flo.

"I'm going to ask Miss Stanley if I can do it right now!" said Charly, running across the playground towards the school buildings.

"So, Miss Stanley," said Charly, breathless from her run back to the classroom where she found their teacher getting things ready for the afternoon lessons. "I thought I could write to Janine and ask her if she's coming back here to visit any time soon. If she is, then I can interview her and write about it for the magazine."

"I think that's a brilliant idea," Miss Stanley said.

"Go Glitter!" said Charly.

Chapter 6

"I think you should phone Mrs James," Flo suggested to Charly when the Glitter Girls were sitting in Meg's bedroom on Saturday afternoon.

"Flo's right!" said Zoe. "Why don't you ring her? Did she put a telephone number on her letter?"

"I don't know," Charly said.

"Here, let's see it," said Hannah.

Charly pulled the letter Mrs James had sent Mrs Wadhurst from her new backpack. It was made of purple bubbly plastic and it was really cool. Hannah took the letter from her friend.

A few minutes later, Charly was standing in the

hallway of Meg's house, the phone in her hand. As she was dialling Mrs James's telephone number, her four best friends were waiting in Meg's bedroom. Charly had asked them not to listen to her on the phone because she was worried in case she said something silly.

Mrs James answered the phone almost straight away.

Charly explained who she was and then asked, "I was wondering if Janine was coming to see you soon because I'd like to interview her for *Wow!*"

Mrs James sounded really excited by the idea and promised to call and ask Janine when she might be back. "Why don't I find out what she says and then get back to you?" she asked Charly.

"OK, great! Thanks, Mrs James!" Charly replied.

"Shall I call you at school or at home?" Mrs James asked.

"School would be OK, I think. Thanks again! Bye!"

Charly raced up the stairs two at a time and burst into Meg's bedroom. She was grinning from ear to ear.

"What did she say?" Zoe asked.

"Was she nice?" Hannah wondered.

"She's going to speak to Janine for us," Charly said. "And yes – she was really friendly! She's going to phone school next week and tell us when Janine is next coming back."

"I hope she's going to come soon enough so that you can get her interview into *Wow!*" Flo said.

Suddenly, Charly looked worried. "That's a point – I should have told Mrs James about the deadline. . ."

"Don't worry, Charly," Meg said, reassuringly. "I'm sure it will be OK."

★ ♥ ★ ♥ ★ ♥ ★

The next meeting for the magazine was at lunchtime on Monday in Miss Stanley's classroom as usual.

"Hello everyone," Miss Stanley said. "I think that today we should really start sorting through the things that have been sent in to *Wow!* Meg, can you find all the letters we've received, please?"

Meg dug out a big pile of envelopes.

"Looks like we've got more than enough already," Ollie said.

"Come on," Miss Stanley said. "Take a couple of envelopes each and then we can sort them more quickly."

"How should we sort them?" Meg asked.

"I think we should organize them in date order," Miss Stanley suggested. "The oldest material can go on the table there and the most up to date over there."

There was a flurry of activity as each of them eagerly looked inside the envelopes and pulled out letters, old photographs and newspaper cuttings.

Miss Stanley put Meg, Amy and Georgios in charge of recording all the information.

"There's something here about a concert that Wells Road choir sang at in France," said Flo.

"This photograph is ancient – it's of the old school building and was taken just after the Second World War," reported Claudia.

Amy, Meg and Georgios busily wrote things down as the other magazine team members read things out to them.

"There's so much here!" sighed Zoe. "Do you think we'll have enough space for it all?"

"We'll do our best to put it all in." Miss Stanley smiled.

"The photos will look great," said Flo. "We'll have to scan all the pictures in – just like they do on the newspaper!"

"Oh!" Meg exclaimed, her hand over her mouth. "We forgot to mention our idea for 'Go Glitter'!"

"What's that?" Miss Stanley asked.

Hannah explained their idea for the make-up and hair question and answer column. There were murmurs of approval from the girls at the meeting. The boys didn't even seem interested so they certainly didn't complain.

"If we can fit it in it sounds good," Miss Stanley confirmed. "Can you organize the questions?"

"No problem," Zoe said.

"Good." Miss Stanley looked at her watch. "It's getting late. I think you'd all better get back to your classrooms for afternoon lessons!"

★　♥　★　♥　★　♥　★

The next few days seemed to go very slowly for Charly. Every morning she woke up wondering if Mrs James would call about Janine. She'd almost given up hope when, on Thursday morning, Miss Stanley handed her a note that was tucked into the class register. It was from

Mrs Packer in the school office. Quickly, Charly opened it. It read,

Charly
Mrs James called. She says that Janine will be here at the weekend. Can you go to see her on Saturday afternoon? Please call and let her know.
Mrs Packer

"Phew!" Charly said loudly.

Everyone turned round. Miss Stanley was halfway through the register when Charly had interrupted!

"I beg your pardon, Charly?" Miss Stanley said, looking a bit cross.

"Oh sorry, Miss Stanley," Charly said. "It's just that I've heard from Janine James's mum. She says I can interview her on Saturday afternoon!"

The Glitter Girls all chattered excitedly, congratulating their friend.

Miss Stanley laughed. "Well done, Charly – it'll be great to have Janine James in *Wow!* But at the moment we'd better get on with the register."

"That's really good news, Charly," whispered Meg, who was sitting next to her at the table.

"Go Glitter!" Zoe, Hannah and Flo mouthed from their own seats.

Charly was so excited she didn't know if she could wait another two days before she saw Janine. At lunchtime, Meg suggested that they meet up after school to help Charly get ready for the interview.

"But I can't come this afternoon," Zoe sighed. "I've got a riding lesson."

"Oh, I'd forgotten – I've got a cello lesson!" said Meg.

"Well, let's meet for tea at my house tomorrow," Charly suggested.

"And you'd better ring Mrs James this evening to tell her that you're coming!" Flo reminded her.

"That we're all coming!" Charly corrected her.
"Go Glitter!" her friends agreed.

★ ♥ ★ ♥ ★ ♥ ★

Hannah, Zoe, Flo and Meg were just as excited as Charly about the thought of meeting Janine. After all, she was the editor of one of their favourite magazines.

"What are you going to ask her first?" Hannah wanted to know, when the Glitter Girls had settled down in Charly's bedroom after school on Friday.

"Well," Charly said, getting out a purple gel pen and her new sequinned folder that was filled with pink paper. "I've obviously got to ask her about when she was at Wells Road School and who her favourite teacher was."

"Good one," agreed Meg. "And perhaps you should ask her who her best friends were?"

"And does she still see them?" said Flo.

Charly busily wrote everything down. "I want

to know how old she was when she decided she wanted to work on a magazine, too."

"Why don't you ask where she went after our school?" suggested Zoe. "I mean, did she go to Jack's school and then college?"

"And is working on *Glitz* her first job?" Flo wanted to know.

"Has she met loads of famous pop stars, do you think?" Hannah wondered.

"I bet she goes to parties and pop concerts every night!" said Meg, remembering all the great CDs she'd been listening to at home for her own piece she was writing for *Wow!*

"Do you think it's non-stop brilliant working on *Glitz*?" Charly said to her friends.

"Well, tomorrow we'll find out!" Meg replied.

"Go Glitter!" they all cheered at once.

Chapter 7

The Glitter Girls could hardly bear to wait until Saturday afternoon. Straight after lunch, they got together in Zoe's bedroom.

"Hey, you look great, Charly!" said Zoe, "I love that top!"

"Thanks – you look good too!"

Charly had chosen to wear a cool pair of pink velvet bootlegs with a sparkling dark pink top and, of course, her denim Glitter Girl jacket.

Zoe was wearing a cute red gypsy skirt and a T-shirt under her jacket.

"I love your combat trousers, Hannah – are they new?" asked Meg, admiring Hannah who was a combination of purple and denim.

"I got them from Girl's Dream," Hannah confirmed. "And I love your dress too!"

Meg was wearing a flowery pink pinafore over a T-shirt that she'd been given for her birthday.

Flo was the last of them to arrive. She'd come straight from a shopping trip with her sister Kim that morning and was wearing orange cropped trousers and a T-shirt that said "Kute" on the front.

"Are we all ready then?" Flo asked.

"Pretty much," Charly said. "But I'm really nervous – do you think Janine will be scary?"

"Shouldn't think so," Meg said. "After all, her mum was really nice on the phone, wasn't she, so she probably is too."

"And," said Zoe, "you're going to have us with you as well!"

"Go Glitter!" the five friends yelled.

Later that afternoon, the Glitter Girls cycled round to Mrs James's house with Zoe's dad.

"I'll come back in about an hour to collect you," Mr Baker said, waving the girls goodbye at the gate.

Leaving their bikes just inside the front garden, the girls made their way to the front door and knocked.

Seconds later it was opened by a tall, dark-haired girl who was wearing baby pink cords and a denim jacket. As soon as she saw the Glitter Girls all wearing their denim jackets too, she said, "Snap! Hi – I guess one of you must be Charly? I'm Janine!"

"I'm Charly. Hello." Charly moved towards the door.

"It's great to meet you, Charly," Janine smiled. "And who are your friends? Apart, of course, from being the Glitter Girls."

Charly quickly introduced them all.

"How do you know about the Glitter Girls?" Zoe asked.

"Ah!" said Janine, grinning. "Your reputation!"

"What?" Flo asked, puzzled.

"I was talking to my mum," Janine explained. "And she told me all the things she's read about you in the paper. Sounds like you're regular action girls!"

The Glitter Girls beamed with pleasure.

"Come on," Janine said. "You'd better come in and we can have our chat."

Charly's chance had finally come!

About an hour later, the Glitter Girls had heard all about Janine's life. They listened to Charly and Janine chat away about how Janine had always got into trouble at school for larking about and how she'd always wanted to work in magazines. She explained that after she'd been to college, she'd got her first job on the local paper, but after a year she'd moved to London to work on a magazine and had eventually worked her way up to become the editor of

Glitz. The Glitter Girls were fascinated to hear about all the famous people that Janine had met through *Glitz*: pop stars, soap stars – even movie actors!

"In fact," Janine told them as Flo was taking her photograph at the end, "there's a boy from Wells Road School who's about to become really famous, you know."

"Who's that?" Charly asked, busily writing everything down in her notebook.

"He's called Darren Dee," Janine explained. "He left about six years ago. I found out about him last week when I had to interview him."

"Darren Dee!" said Meg, excited. "But he's in the final of *Chartbusters*!"

"Yes – I went to talk to him about it," Janine said.

"I'm sure that Darren's going to win!" Zoe exclaimed.

"He's really good!" said Flo.

"And he used to go to our school as well?" Charly asked.

"He certainly did," Janine confirmed.

"That's fantastic," Hannah said. "I was going to ask my mum if I could vote for him anyway, but I've got to now!"

Just then, there was a knock at the door. It was Zoe's dad – he'd come back on his bike to collect the girls.

"Thanks so much, Janine," Charly grinned. "It was really great meeting you."

"No problem," Janine said, putting her arm round Charly. "Just you make sure you send me a copy of *Wow!* when it's printed. Only don't make it look better than *Glitz* or I'll be out of a job!"

★ ♥ ★ ♥ ★ ♥ ★

Charly couldn't wait to get to school on Monday and tell the *Wow!* team about her interview with Janine. But she had to wait until after school because that was the first time they were all together for their meeting. Everyone had reported on their individual projects and now it was time for the Glitter Girls to do the same.

"I've had a really good time listening to all the CDs that I was lent," Meg explained. "I thought I'd decide which one I liked best and do my own chart listing – you know, putting them in order of best to worst."

"That sounds very sensible," Miss Stanley said. "Now, how about you, Charly? Tell us all about Janine James!" she grinned.

"It was fantastic!" Charly beamed, and she went on to tell everyone about Janine and what she'd told them about Darren Dee.

"Cool!" said Amy.

"I love Darren Dee – he's definitely the best on *Chartbusters*," Claudia said.

"He's not bad," Tony and Georgios agreed.

"I've written up my interview, here." Charly had typed up her interview on her computer at home, and she handed it over to Miss Stanley.

"I took some photographs of Janine," Flo explained, "and they'll be developed by the end of the week."

"That's great, girls," said Miss Stanley. "OK, I think we've got enough now to start putting some page designs together. Has anyone else got anything to report?"

"I've nearly finished my 'What's Hot!' column too," Zoe said.

"Well done," Miss Stanley said, ticking her own notes. "What about you, Hannah?"

"We've had some excellent questions in for our 'Go Glitter' column," she explained. "So I just need to choose the ones we're going to put in."

"OK," Miss Stanley said. "There's still a lot more work to be done. "Let's go into the library and start putting things on to the computer. I want to teach Flo to use the scanner so we can insert all the photographs and illustrations we've got so far."

"Yes!" they all yelled enthusiastically.

Chapter 8

The next week went by in a flurry of magazine meetings. Miss Stanley indeed taught Flo how to use the scanner so that she could start getting all the great old photographs ready. It was like a kind of photocopier that made the pictures appear on the computer screen. There were lots of great drawings from the other pupils. But choosing a picture for the front cover of *Wow!* was a problem.

"There's just so many to choose from," Meg sighed when they all met up on Tuesday. They had spread out all the final twenty pictures that had been sent to them by children at school.

"They're all really good though," Claudia said.

"That's the biggest problem," said Flo. "I mean, how do we decide one is better than all the others?"

"Why don't we use a photograph instead of a drawing then?" Zoe suggested.

"Yes," agreed Hannah. "We've had loads sent in, haven't we? How about one of the ones of the old school?"

Meg quickly pulled out a folder and spread the selection of old photographs in front of everyone.

They all looked at them thoughtfully.

"Not very exciting, are they?" Tony said.

"He's right," said Charly. "I mean, they're all really interesting I know, but none of them are really . . . well . . . zappy, are they?"

"No," Miss Stanley said slowly. "None of them are as exciting as the photo of us that appeared in the paper."

"That's it!" said Flo. "The photo in the paper! Why don't we use that?"

"Yes!" There was instant approval from the rest of the team.

"We'd need to check with Sara that we could use it," Miss Stanley said, finding the cutting of the article that Sara had written about them. "But yes, I think that's a really good idea!"

"I'll check it with Sara," Meg said, scribbling a note to herself in her purple notebook.

"Sorted!" said Flo, feeling relieved. Now she could get on with finishing the layout of the last few pages.

★ ♥ ★ ♥ ★ ♥ ★

On Wednesday, Hannah read out the article she had written about doing a makeover on your bedroom. She'd based it on her own bedroom – right down to the fancy cushions and sparkly pink walls.

"Disgusting!" Tony said when she finished.

"That's enough, Tony!" Miss Stanley warned. She could see how upset Hannah was.

"What do you mean?" Meg asked, feeling cross and sorry for her friend at the same time.

"How many boys are going to want to paint their rooms pink?" exclaimed Ollie. The other boys muttered their agreement.

"Oh. . ." Hannah looked down at the drawing she had done to accompany her article and realized that what Tony and the others said was true. Now that she thought about it she should have remembered that boys like Meg's brother Jack wouldn't dream of having a bedroom that looked like hers.

"Well, why don't one of you boys write about decorating a boy's room?" Miss Stanley suggested.

"No way," Ollie said.

"Haven't got time," said Tony. The other boys felt the same.

"OK then, I'll write about a boy's room," Hannah said.

"What do you know about it?" Georgios said.

"Not a lot at the moment, but I reckon I could find out," Hannah replied confidently.

"If you lot are so clever, tell us what you'd want in your bedroom if you were redecorating then!" said Charly.

"Easy peasy," Tony said. Then between them, the boys explained all the things that they'd do while Hannah made notes on everything they said.

"Right then," she said when they'd finished. "I'll write about that tonight!"

"Thank you, Hannah," Miss Stanley said, looking at her list. "Now, Amy – can you tell us how you've got on?"

And the meeting continued.

★ ♥ ★ ♥ ★ ♥ ★

Of course, Hannah wrote a brilliant piece about boys' bedrooms and even Tony, Ollie and Georgios had to agree that they rather fancied having a bedroom that looked like the one that

Hannah had drawn in her picture. Hannah showed her work to the magazine team in their meeting on Thursday at lunchtime.

It was a good meeting, and Meg was pleased to report that almost all the material was now in from all the individual reporters, including her own piece about the CD reviews and chart report. Sue had done a brilliant crossword too. Claudia had found out about everyone's achievements and the "Where are they now?" page was one they had all worked on and everyone was really pleased with it. Even Ollie had finished his fashion page, ahead of Amy's.

"I'll have it done by tomorrow, promise," Amy said, irritated that Ollie had beaten her.

"I'll have 'What's Hot!' done by then too," Zoe confirmed.

"Here's my football report," said Georgios.

"What's happened to the recipe, Tony?" Meg asked, ticking things off on her list.

"Got it here!" Tony said, as he placed a piece of paper in front of Meg.

"Hey, this looks great!" Meg said as she read it.

"What's it for?" Hannah asked.

"Chocolate muffin cake," Tony grinned. "And it's very chocolatey!"

"Sounds delicious!" everyone agreed, feeling hungry for their tea even though they'd only just eaten lunch.

"Hey, you lot," Charly whispered to her best friends as she glanced at the recipe. "Do you think we could bake this for tea this afternoon?"

"Good idea," said Meg. "We should probably make sure it's all correct before we put it in the magazine anyway."

"Go Glitter!"

That afternoon, the Glitter Girls went back to Charly's house.

"Mum," Charly said, when they were driving home. "Can we do some cooking when we get in?"

"What kind of cooking?" Mrs Fisher asked.

"Well, we've got this great chocolate cake recipe for *Wow!* and we wondered if we could try it out?"

"It sounds delicious," Flo confirmed. "Chocolate muffin cake!"

"That does sound good," Mrs Fisher agreed. "OK, you're on. But you must call me when you need to put the cake in and take it out of the oven so I can do it for you."

"Go Glitter!" the five best friends agreed.

"And you've got to let me have a slice of cake too!"

★ ♥ ★ ♥ ★ ♥ ★

Later on, in the kitchen, the Glitter Girls worked as a team. Meg read out the ingredients and Flo and Hannah measured them on the scales.

It was Charly and Zoe who did the mixing. Mrs Fisher had told them that they had to tie their hair back and then put on aprons after they'd washed their hands. But there were five of them and only two aprons – so in the end they had to make do with tea towels wrapped around their middles!

"I think you should all have a go at stirring the cake before it goes in the tin," Mrs Fisher suggested. "Maybe you should make a wish too!"

"I wish that *Wow!* is the best magazine ever!" said Hannah.

"Yes!" her friends agreed.

When they'd all had a go at stirring, Charly carefully poured the cake mixture into the tin that Meg had lined and then they watched as Mrs Fisher placed the cake in the oven.

"When's it going to be ready?" Meg asked impatiently, as they all helped with the washing up.

"It's been in the oven for nearly half an hour already!" said Hannah.

"And it smells great!" sighed Charly, feeling peckish.

"OK – I'll check it for you!" Mrs Fisher grinned, putting the mixing bowl away.

Charly's mum took the cake from the oven and put it on a wire rack to cool a little. It looked as delicious as it smelled.

"It's certainly cooked," Mrs Fisher said, gently touching the top of the cake. "But you can't eat it yet! You'll have to wait at least another half an hour for it to cool down."

★ ♥ ★ ♥ ★ ♥ ★

It seemed more like an hour to the Glitter Girls as they sat in the kitchen watching the great fat chocolate cake cooling on the wire rack. But eventually, Mrs Fisher said it had cooled enough for her to cut the cake and she gave each of them a slice.

"Me first!" they all cried and Mrs Fisher laughed as she cut the last slice. "OK – now you can eat it!" she said.

The Glitter Girls tucked in eagerly.

"Yuck!"

"Disgusting!"

"Urghh!"

"Whatever's wrong?" Mrs Fisher asked.

"Taste it!" Charly said, pulling a face. "It's horrible!"

Mrs Fisher took a crumb from Charly's plate and nibbled on it.

"Hmm, the chocolate is quite strong," Mrs Fisher said. "And it's quite bitter."

"But it doesn't taste like cake, does it?" Zoe said.

Mrs Fisher thought for a while.

"Are you sure you didn't miss anything out when you wrote down Tony's recipe?" Mrs Fisher wondered, picking up the sheet of paper from the worktop.

"Course," said Meg. "But I don't suppose Tony's dad sells cakes like this in his tea room."

"No. . ." Mrs Fisher was busy reading the recipe the girls had worked from. "Actually," she said when she'd finished. "I think I've spotted where it's gone wrong."

"What?" Flo asked.

"Sugar!" Mrs Fisher laughed. "Tony forgot to write down how much sugar to include. You don't get many chocolate cakes without sugar, you know!"

"Trust Tony!" Zoe said.

"Yes – we should take this in to school to make him eat it!" Hannah said.

"Never mind, girls," Mrs Fisher said. "It's just a good job you checked the recipe before you put it in *Wow!* Come on – let's find some of my chocolate brownies for you. Maybe that will make you feel better."

"Go Glitter!"

Chapter 9

It was Friday breaktime and the Glitter Girls were telling the others in the magazine team about the chocolate cake disaster.

"So it was a good job we checked it out!" Meg giggled.

"Sorry," Tony said. "But it's a really good cake if you put the sugar in!"

Everyone laughed.

"OK, gang," Miss Stanley said. "We've only got one more week to go and Sara said that she would try to pop in this morning to see how we are getting on. While we wait for her though, we'd better get on. Meg, what's left to come in?"

Meg read through the list. Amy and Zoe

handed over their articles that they had promised the day before.

"That only leaves the 'Go Glitter' column and Flo's photographs from Charly's interview with Janine," Meg reported.

"Excellent," Miss Stanley said. "Flo, how have you got on with the design of the pages?"

Before she could answer, there was a knock on the classroom door. It was Sara.

"Hi, everyone!" she smiled. "I just thought I'd come in to find out how it's all going. Is there anything I can look at?"

"You've come just at the right time to see Flo's pages," Meg said.

"Great!" said Sara, sitting down next to Flo.

The next fifteen minutes were spent checking things. Sara gave Flo some ideas about how to make things clearer in places and suggestions on how to make certain things stand out a bit more by using different types of lettering and colours.

"It's all looking fantastic," Sara said. "You've worked really hard since I last saw you."

"Actually," Meg said. "I was going to phone you to check if we can use the photograph of us from the paper for the front cover of *Wow!*" She showed the cover mock-up to Sara.

"That looks really cool!" Sara agreed. "I'm sure you can use it – but you'd probably better make sure you say that it was Kevin who took the photograph and mention the paper too!"

"OK," Meg said, writing it down in her notebook.

Just then, Mrs Wadhurst rushed into the room.

"Goodness, I'm glad I caught you before lessons begin again," she said. "I've just had a phone call from Janine James. She's managed to get hold of some VIP tickets for the *Chartbusters* final and she wondered if you can all go along with her tomorrow to see it, so you can write about it for *Wow!*"

"Yes!!!" the whole room screamed.

"I'll need to phone all your parents though and check that you're allowed to go," Mrs Wadhurst warned. "Miss Stanley and I could go with you if they say yes. We could get the train to London."

The room was a buzz of noise. All of them desperately hoped that they'd be allowed to go.

"You lucky things!" Sara said. "I wish I could go. Still, any chance I can have a copy of the article you write? Then I can put it in the news-paper too!"

"Go Glitter!" the five best friends screamed.

And this time everyone else – even Miss Stanley and Mrs Wadhurst – joined them!

★ ♥ ★ ♥ ★ ♥ ★

The Glitter Girls could hardly believe their luck! Only last weekend, they had watched *Chartbusters* on television and now they were getting the chance to be in the audience at the final!

"Do you think Darren Dee will win?" Charly wondered.

The Glitter Girls had met up in Hannah's bedroom to help each other choose what they should wear.

"It would be great if he did!" said Meg.

"I'm going to take my camera," Flo said. "In case I get the chance to take a photo of him!"

"Do you think I'll look OK in this?" Charly asked, holding up a pink T-shirt that had darker pink stars all over it.

"What are you going to wear it with?" Zoe wondered.

"My jeans and this cap," Charly explained.

"Great!" said Hannah. "I'm going to wear my purple top and pink skirt."

"I'm going to wear my purple top too!" Zoe said. "You know the one with the lines of stars on? And I've got this great new purple rose to put in my hair too."

"Snap!" said Meg. "I'm wearing purple too! I think I'll go for my purple combats and a glittery purple top. What about you, Flo?"

"I thought I'd wear my new T-shirt with the pink swirls on," she explained. "It looks really cool with my jeans."

"I just can't wait to get there!" Meg sighed.

"Nor can I," agreed Hannah.

"Doing *Wow!* has been really good, hasn't it?" said Charly.

"Go Glitter!" agreed her friends.

Chapter 10

The journey to London seemed to take for ever. When they did get there, Janine met them at the station.

"Hi gang!" she smiled. "Listen – I've arranged for a mini-bus to take us to the *Chartbusters* studios."

"Wow!" they all said, grinning with excitement.

"Oh," said Janine. "And the other thing is that I wondered if you'd like a trip around the *Glitz* office on the way?"

The Glitter Girls looked at each other excitedly. VIP tickets to *Chartbusters* and a trip round the offices of their favourite mag. Could the day get any better?!

The rest of the group – even the boys – were almost as excited as the Glitter Girls. They all piled into the mini-bus.

★ ♥ ★ ♥ ★ ♥ ★

The *Glitz* office was fantastic. Janine explained that no one was working there that day because it was a Saturday. But she took them on a whistle-stop tour of all the departments. It was just like the newspaper trip – only this time the walls were covered with signed photographs of pop stars and soap actors. And there was also a great walk-in wardrobe full of clothes that had been sent in for fashion shoots. The Glitter Girls weren't the only ones who wished they could stay longer, but Janine warned them that they had to hurry to the studios to make sure they got their seats.

The television studio was just as busy as the one the Glitter Girls had been to for the ChariTV telethon.

Suddenly the lights were dimmed.

"This is so exciting!" Meg said, squeezing Zoe's hand as they settled into their seats.

"It's starting!" Charly said, sitting back in her seat and concentrating. She wanted to make sure she remembered every minute of the show so that she could put it all in *Wow!*

Over the next two hours, the Glitter Girls and all of their school friends who'd worked on *Wow!* sat riveted to their seats. *Chartbusters* was one of the most fantastic things they had ever seen. Especially since they had all been watching, week by week, following tonight's finalists. Everyone they saw was brilliant; the girl singers in their gorgeous outfits, the boy singers who were cool and cute. Darren Dee was just great – but was he going to be chosen as the winner in the end?

As they were all still pondering on who would

win, the director of the show stopped the recording and explained to the audience that there would be a wait while the judges considered their decision.

"Wasn't that great?" Charly sighed when the lights went up.

"Fantastic!" said Meg.

"Hey, look – isn't that the lead singer from Fabulosa over there?" said Hannah.

The others looked round to where she was pointing.

"Yes – I think you're right!" said Miss Stanley.

"Are you enjoying this, everyone?" Mrs Wadhurst asked.

Yes!" they all agreed at once, and carried on looking for more famous people in the audience.

When it was time for the winner to be announced the tension was almost unbearable.

The Glitter Girls all wanted Darren to win. He was definitely the best (and the cutest!) and they had to support him – he'd been at their school, after all!

The audience waited expectantly as one of the presenters read out this year's winner of *Chartbusters*. . . It was Darren Dee!

The girls hugged each other in their excitement – they were so glad he'd won!

"I can't believe a boy from Wells Road School won *Chartbusters*!" Mrs Wadhurst said as they stood up to leave their seats following Darren's final performance.

"I wish we could go and congratulate him on winning!" Charly said.

"Well, that's where I can help!" said Janine.

"How?" Hannah asked.

"Because I had a word with Darren earlier and told him all about you guys and that you were here, and he asked if you could come along and see him after the show!"

The Glitter Girls couldn't believe it! Nor could their friends!

"Come on," said Janine, ushering them all down the aisle towards the entrance to backstage. "If we don't go now, we'll miss our chance!"

Darren seemed really happy to see them. "I've heard all about your magazine," he said. "Can I be in it?"

"You bet!" said Meg.

"Can I have your autograph?" Georgios asked.

"Sure," Darren said, and before long he was busy signing lots of bits of paper because everyone wanted his autograph!

"Can I take some photos?" Flo asked.

"No problem!" Darren smiled.

As Flo clicked away with her camera, Charly asked Darren some questions. Had he liked school? Did he sing a solo in the school concert? When did he decide he'd like to be a pop star? Would he come back to school when he was famous to sing for them? When was his first record coming out?

"Isn't this great?" Charly asked Zoe as they settled back in their seats a few minutes later.

"Fantastic!" said Zoe. "I can't believe we've met Darren Dee! Just imagine how cool this will look once we put it in *Wow!*"

★ ❤ ★ ❤ ★ ❤ ★

"Sorry to cut the evening short, everyone – but we've got to get the train home and I'm sure Darren's got plenty of people he needs to see and celebrate with!" Miss Stanley said.

The group gathered together and they found their way out of the studios, where the mini-bus was waiting for them.

"Janine – thank you so much for a great day." said Miss Stanley.

"Yes, thanks!" everyone called.

"It was fantastic," said Charly.

"Glad you enjoyed it," said Janine. "Now – you guys have a safe journey home and make sure you send me a copy of *Wow!* when it's out!"

"We will!" said Meg.

"And Flo," Janine said. "Why don't I take the film from your camera. I'll get it developed at the magazine over the weekend and then I can e-mail you the results. Then you'll get them in time for *Wow!*"

"Thanks Janine!" Flo said, handing the film over.

"Come on, everyone," Mrs Wadhurst said. "We don't want to miss the train!"

"Bye!" they all called.

"See you!" Janine waved.

School would have seemed really boring on Monday after their *Chartbusters* adventure if it hadn't been for the fact that they had to put the final touches on the magazine.

"I finished typing up my interview yesterday," Charly explained at breaktime.

"And Meg, Hannah, Flo and I worked on the 'Go Glitter' column," Zoe said.

"Now we just need the photos from Janine," Flo said.

"OK," said Meg. "Why don't we see if Mrs Packer has had any e-mails from Janine?"

The rest of the Glitter Girls agreed and the five of them trooped off to the school office.

"I expect you've come for these," said Mrs Packer, who had printed out some things for them.

"Hey!" Charly beamed. "They are fantastic!"

They were, too. Mrs Packer had printed off Flo's photographs and she had taken some great ones.

"And look at this!" Zoe said.

Janine had used a photo taken of Charly that night to mock up a *Glitz* cover. Charly was a *Glitz* cover girl – how cool was that?!

"Oh!" Charly exclaimed, overwhelmed with excitement.

Just then, Miss Stanley came out of the staff room.

"What have you got there, girls?" she asked.

They handed her the photos.

"These are great!" Miss Stanley exclaimed. Then she spotted the cover. "Well, Charly. I think this is something for your bedroom wall, don't you? You should get it framed!"

★　♥　★　♥　★　♥　★

The next two days were busier than ever. They had to add extra pages to the magazine to make sure they could include Charly's report on *Chartbusters*. Everyone on the magazine team worked really hard. Flo designed the final pages and the others checked through them, looking for spelling mistakes and anything that was missing. *Wow!* absolutely had to be ready for Thursday. And that included getting it photo-copied and handing it round to all the classrooms. It was a frantic rush on Wednesday lunchtime as they had their last meeting. But on Thursday morning, the magazine team came in early to put all the pages in the right order and staple them together. They were finished at breaktime.

"I think we've done it!" said Meg.

"I thought we never would," admitted Georgios.

"And it's looking so great!" said Amy.

Everyone agreed with her.

"Let's go and see Mrs Wadhurst," Miss Stanley said, grinning. "I told her we'd bring it to her in her office when we were ready."

Between them, the group carried the bundles of magazines along the corridor.

"Hello," Mrs Wadhurst said, greeting them at her office door. "Is it finished at last?"

"After a great deal of hard work from my excellent editorial team it is indeed finished, Mrs Wadhurst!" Miss Stanley smiled, handing her a copy from the top of the pile that Charly was carrying.

"Doesn't it look great?" said Mrs Wadhurst as she flicked through it. "Right, come on you lot. We're just in time to hand them out for assembly!"

Between them, the editorial team made sure that every class had a pile of magazines.

"I'm sure that you will all agree that Miss Stanley and her editorial team have made a great job of putting together *Wow!*" Mrs Wadhurst said. "In fact – why don't we give them all a cheer! Stand up all you *Wow!* people!"

Around the hall, boys and girls stood up and smiled as the rest of the school cheered them on.

After assembly, Miss Stanley asked the Glitter Girls and their friends who'd been involved in the magazine to help clear up the office they'd used as a base for creating *Wow!*

Miss Stanley said she'd meet them all back there. When Charly opened the door though, they were greeted by balloons and streamers and Miss Stanley and Sara saying, "Congratulations!"

Sara had brought along a huge cake that was decorated with lettering the same as that they'd used on the magazine. It read *Wow!* in big red letters, made out of delicious icing!

"We thought you deserved a bit of a party seeing as you all worked so hard," explained Miss Stanley.

The Glitter Girls and their friends were totally surprised and really happy that they had a way to celebrate the success of *Wow!*

"This is fab!" said Charly, beaming.

"Yes, brilliant," said Flo, through a mouthful of cake.

"Thanks, Miss Stanley," Amy added.

"By the way, Charly, do you have a copy of the article you wrote about *Chartbusters* for me?" Sara asked.

"You bet!" Charly replied, handing her a copy of the magazine. "It's here in your very own copy of *Wow!*"

"Great! It'll be in next week's issue of the paper along with some more copy about the magazine," Sara explained.

"Hurray!" said Charly. "That'll give me something to look forward to – seeing my name in print in the paper!"

"I know it's been loads of hard work," said Miss Stanley, coming over to join the girls and Sara, "but have you all enjoyed it?"

"Absolutely!" said Zoe happily.

"It's been terrific," Meg agreed.

"Go Glitter!" said Hannah.

And this time, everyone joined in!

Don't miss:

Photo Fame

The Glitter Girls are super-excited. They've just heard about auditions for a toothpaste advert and are desperate to take part. . .

The girls come up with their own routine that's sure to get them noticed. Imagine – the Glitter Girls as the face of a fab new toothpaste! They'll be on TV and on billboards all over the country; the Glitter Girls will be famous!